Over the snow, the world is hushed and white.

But under the snow is a secret world of
squirrels and snow hares,
bears and bullfrogs,
and many other animals
who live through the winter
safe and warm
under the snow.

Praise for *Over and Under the Snow*

An ALA Notable Book
A *New York Times* Notable Children's Picture Book
A *New York Times* Editors' Choice
A Bank Street College of Education Best Book of the Year Reading List selection
A Capitol Choices Final Reading List selection

"Calm, lovely and richly informative." —*The New York Times*

"Christopher Silas Neal's illustrations give a nostalgic feel to Kate Messner's
gently lyrical text. . . ."—*The Wall Street Journal*

"*Over and Under the Snow* will make a wonderful book for adults and children
to snuggle with on a cold, snowy day." —*San Francisco Book Review*

★ "This lovely study of the ways animals spend the winter in a 'secret kingdom under the snow'
combines Messner's graceful prose with debut illustrator Neal's quiet, woodcut-like
portraits of the snowy forest." —*Publishers Weekly*, starred review

★ "Beautifully rendered through Messner's sparc, poetic words and Neal's block-print-looking
mixed-media illustrations." —*The Horn Book Magazine*, starred review

★ "This book depicting beauty in nature is a gem. . . ." —*Library Media Connection*, starred review

"Utterly charming, and informative, to boot; readers brought up on a diet of rhymes,
bright colors and adorable fluffy animals will find its simple beauty a balm." —*Kirkus Reviews*

"A good choice for winter reading, this quiet but eye-opening picture book
could heighten a child's awareness of the natural world." —*Booklist*

*For my sister, Anne, who has always left amazing tracks
for me to follow —K. M.*

To Dadavee —C. S. N.

First paperback edition published in 2014 by Chronicle Books LLC.
Originally published in hardcover in 2011 by Chronicle Books LLC.

The Library of Congress has cataloged the hardcover edition as follows:
Messner, Kate.
  Over and under the snow / by Kate Messner.
    p. cm.
  Includes bibliographical references.
  ISBN 978-0-8118-6784-9
  1. Animals—Wintering—Juvenile literature. I. Title.
  QL753.M475 2010
  591.4'3—dc22
  2009028984

ISBN 978-1-4521-3646-2

Manufactured in China.

Design by Amelia Mack.
Typeset in Jannon Antiqua.
The illustrations in this book were rendered in mixed media.

20 19 18 17 16 15 14

Chronicle Books LLC
680 Second Street
San Francisco, California 94107

Chronicle Books—we see things differently.
Become part of our community at www.chroniclekids.com.

Over
and
Under
the Snow

by Kate Messner with art by Christopher Silas Neal

chronicle books · san francisco

Over the snow I glide. Into woods,
frosted fresh and white.

Over the snow, a flash of fur—a red squirrel disappears down a crack.

"Where did he go?"

"Under the snow," Dad says.

"Under the snow is a whole secret kingdom, where the smallest forest animals stay safe and warm. You're skiing over them now."

Over the snow I glide, past beech trees rattling leftover leaves and strong, silent pines that stretch to the sky. On a high branch, a great horned owl keeps watch.

Under the snow, a tiny shrew dodges columns of ice; it follows a cool tunnel along the moss, out of sight.

"Look," Dad says. "Tracks. Tracks always tell a story."

Over the snow, a deer has crossed our path. Deep hoof prints punch through the crust, up the hill, under a tree. An oval of melted snow tells the story of a good night's sleep.

Under the snow, deer mice doze. They huddle up, cuddle up against the cold in a nest of feathers and fur.

Over the snow I climb, digging in my edges so
I don't slide back down.

Under the snow, voles scratch through slippery
tunnels, searching for morsels from summer feasts.

Over the snow I swoosh—

down, down, *faster, faster,*

down, *faster, faster,*

whoops!

Under the snow, a snowshoe hare watches from a shelter of spruce. Almost invisible, she smooths her fur—a coat of winter white.

Over the snow I glide, past reeds where tadpoles play tag in springtime.

Under the snow, fat bullfrogs snooze. They dream of sun-warmed days, back when they had tails.

Over the snow I stand and stare. Little mountains in the marsh.

Under the snow, beavers gnaw on aspen bark, settled in for supper. Can they hear my tummy rumbling, too?

Over the snow—stop. A sound.

We stand like statues carved in ice till a bushy-tailed
fox steps from a thicket. Tips his ear to the ground.

listens . . .

listens . . .

listens still . . .

and L^eaps

out onto the snow after an invisible dinner.

His paws scratch away to find the mouse he heard scritch-scritch-scratching along underneath. Under the snow.

Over the snow I glide. A full moon lights my path to supper.

Under the snow, a chipmunk wakes for a meal. Bedroom, kitchen, hallway—his house under my feet.

Over the snow I climb one last hill. Bonfire smoke rises: warm hands, hot cocoa, hot dogs sizzling on pointed sticks.

Under the snow, a black bear snores, still full of October blueberries and trout.

Over the snow, the fire crackles, and sparks shoot up to the stars. I lick sticky marshmallow from my lips and lean back with heavy eyes. Shadows dance in the flames.

Under the snow, a queen bumblebee drowses
away December, all alone. She'll rule a new
colony in spring.

Over the snow I glide home on tired legs.
Clouds whisper down feathery-soft flakes.

Under the covers, I snuggle deep and drift into dreams . . .

of cuddling deer mice and slumbering frogs. Hungry beavers and tunneling voles. Drowsy bears and busy squirrels. And the secret kingdom under the snow.

Author's Note

There really is a "secret kingdom under the snow." Scientists call it the subnivean zone. It's a network of small open spaces and tunnels between the snowpack and the ground. It's created when heat from the ground melts some of the snow next to it and leaves a layer of air just above the dirt and fallen leaves.

Many animals depend on the subnivean zone to survive the winter. For one thing, the snow acts like the insulation in our houses and keeps the subnivean zone close to 32° Fahrenheit even when the air outside is much colder. Small rodents like mice, moles, and voles travel under the snow because it helps keep them safe from predators—animals like hawks that would like to eat them.

Some predators get tricky, though. Weasels have skinny bodies and can squeeze into the tunnels in search of prey. Red foxes, like the one in this story, have fantastic hearing. They listen carefully for noises under the snow and can figure out just when and where to pounce to collapse the tunnel and trap a mouse for a meal.

If you go cross-country skiing or snowshoeing in the woods, you might see tracks in the snow that lead to tree trunks or crevices and then disappear. Look carefully. Those tracks probably tell the story of an animal from the subnivean zone—that secret kingdom under the snow.

The animals you met in this book really do eat, sleep, hide, and play over and under the winter snow.

Red squirrels not only travel and hide under the snow but also store food underground. They hide seeds and nuts in holes or under rocks and use their fantastic sense of smell to find them later when they're hungry.

Shrews are little animals like mice that sometimes become meals for great horned owls and other predators, so subnivean tunnels provide important shelter.

White-tailed deer like to sleep under coniferous trees (evergreens with cones) that provide shelter on winter nights. When they curl up to sleep, some of the snow underneath them melts, making deer beds easy to spot in the woods.

Deer mice make nests out of grasses, leaves, and other bits of plants and line them with soft moss, fur, and feathers. Mice often sleep huddled together in winter to conserve heat.

Voles look a lot like fat mice but with shorter tails and smaller ears and eyes. Like mice and shrews, voles forage for food under the snow, searching for seeds, bark, roots, and insects.

Snowshoe hares are famous for their seasonal color change. In the summer, these hares have a coat that's reddish brown or gray, but as winter approaches, they shed that hair and replace it with white hair to blend in with the snow. That makes it much easier for the snowshoe hare to hide from predators.

Bullfrogs hibernate, buried in the mud at the bottom of ponds and marshes in the wintertime. Did you know that you can tell the difference between a male bullfrog and a female bullfrog by the size of their tympanum? (That's a fancy word for ear!) On a male bullfrog, the ear is about twice the size of the eye, while a female bullfrog's ear is about the same size as her eye.

Beavers don't hibernate in winter, but they're less active, so they don't need as much food. Whole families spend the coldest months huddled together inside their frozen lodges. Before winter sets in, beavers pile branches and twigs at the bottom of the pond, not far from the entrance to the lodge. That serves as their winter food supply, and they'll dive down under the ice when it's time to eat.

Red foxes often eat small mammals like mice, voles, and shrews, but finding those animals can be challenging in winter. The red fox has an excellent sense of hearing, though, and will actually listen for the sounds of animals like mice under the snow. When a fox hears a mouse, it will pounce, often with all four feet on one spot, to collapse the snow and trap the mouse underneath. Then it will dig until it finds its dinner.

Chipmunks dig burrows in the earth and live there, under the snow, in the wintertime. A chipmunk's home often has different chambers—one for sleeping, one for storing food, and several tunnels for exiting and entering the burrow.

Black bears sleep most of the winter. Before they go to sleep, they gorge themselves on foods like fish and berries so they'll have enough energy to last until spring. Their dens might be in hollowed out trees, under logs or rocks, or in caves.

Bumblebees don't all survive winter in cold climates. In fact, males and worker bees die in the fall, leaving only fertilized queen bees alive. The queen bumblebees hibernate in the soil or under a layer of leaves. They can even produce their own antifreeze to keep from freezing if temperatures drop too low. When the queen emerges in spring, she'll find a cool, dark place to nest (often an abandoned mouse den) and lay her eggs to start a new colony.

Further Reading

If you'd like to know more about animals in winter, you might enjoy the following resources:

Books:

Bancroft, Henrietta. *Animals in Winter*. Harper Collins, 1997.

Barrett George, Lindsay. *In the Snow: Who's Been Here?* Greenwillow, 1999.

Crossingham, John. *What Is Hibernation?* Crabtree Publishing Co., 1997.

Ellis Selsam, Millicent. *Big Tracks, Little Tracks: Following Animal Prints*. Harper Collins, 1998.

Fleming, Denise. *Time to Sleep*. Henry Holt & Co., 2001.

Web Sites:

The University of Michigan Museum of Zoology Animal Diversity Web http://animaldiversity.ummz.umich.edu/site/index.html

Hinterland Who's Who from the Canadian Wildlife Service http://www.hww.ca/index_e.asp

Further Reading for Parents & Teachers:

Heinrich, Bernd. *Winter World: The Ingenuity of Animal Survival*. Ecco, 2003

Kate Messner is a middle school teacher and the author of several books for young readers, including *The Brilliant Fall of Gianna Z.*, the Marty McGuire series, and the Sea Monster series. She lives on Lake Champlain with her family and loves skating on the frozen lake, reading by the fire, and cross-country skiing in the woods. She wrote the first draft of this book on a bumpy school bus, returning from a snowshoe field trip in the Adirondacks. Visit Kate at www.katemessner.com.

Christopher Silas Neal is an award-winning illustrator whose work has been published in a variety of magazines and books and featured on television. He is a regular contributor to the *New York Times* and shows his art at various galleries nationwide. He currently lives and works in Brooklyn and teaches illustration at Pratt Institute.